Joseph
Had a Little
Overcoat

He wore the coat for a long time and then something happened to it.

(and there's a moral, too!)

Simms Taback

SCHOLASTIC INC.
New York Toronto London Auckland Sydney
Mexico City New Delhi Hong Kong

OKTE
GRADE 1
LIBRARY

Dedicated to
Alex Cohen

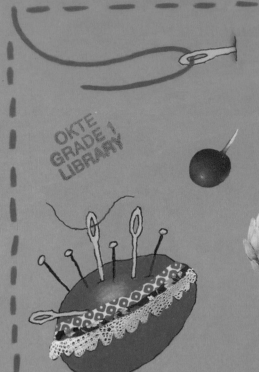

The artwork was done
using watercolor, Gouache,
pencil, ink and collage.

ISBN 0-439-21697-4

Copyright © 1999 by Simms Taback. All rights reserved.
Published by Scholastic Inc., 555 Broadway, New York, NY 10012,
by arrangement with Viking Children's Books, a division of
Penguin Putnam Inc. SCHOLASTIC and associated logos are
trademarks and/or registered trademarks of Scholastic Inc.

12 11 10 9 8 7 6 5 4 3   0 1 2 3 4 5/0

Printed in Mexico   49

First Scholastic printing, September 2000

All lettering designed by Simms Taback

So he made a ja

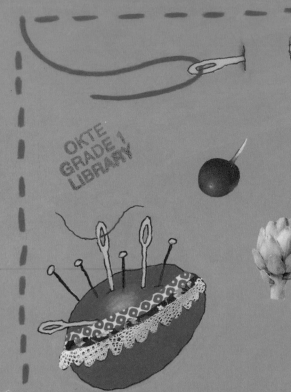

OKTE
GRADE 1
LIBRARY

Dedicated to
Alex Cohen

The artwork was done
using watercolor, Gouache,
pencil, ink and collage.

ISBN 0-439-21697-4

Copyright © 1999 by Simms Taback. All rights reserved.
Published by Scholastic Inc., 555 Broadway, New York, NY 10012,
by arrangement with Viking Children's Books, a division of
Penguin Putnam Inc. SCHOLASTIC and associated logos are
trademarks and/or registered trademarks of Scholastic Inc.

12 11 10 9 8 7 6 5 4 3   0 1 2 3 4 5/0

Printed in Mexico   49

First Scholastic printing, September 2000

All lettering designed by Simms Taback

and went to the fair.

Joseph had a little jacket. It got old and worn.

and danced at his nephew's wedding.

Joseph had a little scarf. It got old and worn.

So he made a necktie out of it

and went to visit his married sister in the city.

Joseph had a little necktie. It got old and worn.

and drank a glass of hot tea with lemon.

Joseph had a little button. One day he lost it.

Now he had nothing.

What one has,
one doesn't want,
and what one wants,
one doesn't have.

you can always make something out of nothing.

Dear Readers,

   As a child I had a favorite song - a yiddish folk song called "I Had a Little Overcoat." Many years ago, I adapted the song to make a book and I called it <u>Joseph Had a Little Overcoat</u>. Some people noticed that Joseph looked a lot like me.

   Now you know that no artist is ever satisfied with his work, but usually we don't get to do it over. So I am particularly happy to be publishing this newly illustrated version of Joseph. I hope that all of you who wrote to me about the early version will take this one to your hearts. That would prove that "you can always make something out of nothing"... over and over again!

Simms Taback